WEIRD AND WACKY ANTHOLOGY

VOLUME ONE

IMA GHOUL

The Written Word Publishing

Australia

Contact: keltoidrui@hotmail.com

https://nadineabrahams.wixsite.com/author

ISBN: 978-0-646-87624-5 (Paperback) 978-1-7643944-1-3 (ebook)

Contents

The Newcomer

S imon grinned broadly down at his fiancée donned in an ugly Christmas sweater despite the scorching weather. The hot Australian sun had reached its pinnacle, perched high above the scalding and cracked earth; a cold-hearted phenomenon in a cloudless blue sky reminiscent of clear water on a balmy day. The vestiges of green on leaves, withered and parched, lay wilted in the boughs of native eucalyptus while fauna sought shade or became stealthy poachers sipping H20 from containers left out for pets.

'It's really hot. Are you sure you won't take that off?'

'This is mild in comparison from where I spawned.'

'You really are odd.' Simon laughed and exhaled through pursed lips, hot breath mildly cooling the damp brown hair plastered to his forehead, before knocking on the wooden door.

'Coming,' a deep familiar voice boomed while heavy, booted feet thudded towards the opposing side of the door.

Simon leant down and pressed a kiss to his fiancée's brow. 'They will love you.'

The door was pulled open. A middle-aged man with spectacles perched on his pointed nose, locked eyes with Simon before daring a glance at the newcomer. 'Hello, son. Is this the fiancée?'

Simon gave his father a vigorous nod. 'Yes, Father.'

'Hmmmm.' The older man leant towards the newcomer, eyes pivoted on their guest's as if peering into their soul. 'Name?'

'Father, you are being … unusual.' Simon laughed nervously.

'Oh right, right.' The bespectacled man drew back. 'I am zgau—'

'What my father means to say is … ' Simon stepped towards the portal that would allow them access to his sire's abode.

The older man coughed. 'Forgive me, I choked. My name is Alistair Zgaun. What name did you claim?'

The older man began to walk through the entry as the couple followed.

'Father, my fiancée is called Venus Zorp.' Simon hurried after his sire.

'Unusual name.' Alistair turned towards the invited pair, gesturing to the fluorescent green walls. 'As you can see, we are a standard family. My walls are adorned with likenesses of our family unit in mundane tasks.' Their host attempted a grin, which was more of a grimace. 'Now, you shall be accosted by kith and kin making merry while we have plucked a living evergreen and festooned it with homemade baubles, and imbibe toxins to fuel unacknowledged grudges.'

'Thank you for inviting me to engage in your festivities.' Venus bowed at the waist.

They entered the room. A Christmas tree was dressed haphazardly as if it was an afterthought. Roughly carved wooden baubles, bearing no paint to gladden up or accentuate its raw design, followed a theme of iconic Christmas novelties such as stars, deer and snowmen. The ceiling exploded in too much popcorn and dried cranberry threaded on strings, red and white rings of crepe paper made into garlands and garish vintage decorations hung from above.

The furniture was minimalist, a large table to the back of the room near a glass door, a vinyl couch near the back room poised to offer comforts as you crossed the grey linoleum floor.

Several women of middling and adolescent years surged forwards as if engaged in battle, their voices rose in a cacophony reminiscent of a banshee as questions were hurled at the pair, cheeks were pinched, the air was squeezed from them as they were embraced before the gaggle of aunties, nannas, cousins and mums retreated, their conquest won.

The women, having greeted the pair accordingly, sidled away to prepare the afternoon repast, leaving the masculine entities and their small replicas to terrorize the couple, from Uncle Peter sporting several beers adorned with rosy cheeks and yeasty breath to shake Simon's hand and press a kiss to Venus's cheek, to Grandpa Bruce commenting on the solid weather while the nippers demanded attention by pulling on garments and howling statements of, 'pick me up and what did you bring me'.

'Oh hello.' Venus greeted the menfolk and took a step back. 'Oh yes, the weather is accurate for one of the four segregated changes in atmosphere.' She laughed nervously. 'No, I don't imbue in alcohol.' Venus held their hands up in protest as Peter pushed a can of beer into the guest's hand.

The matriarch of the abode stepped out from the kitchen, armed with tongs, donned in a festive hat, a checkered apron guarding her garments from splatter, a half-full wine glass in her left hand.

'Eeek.' The matriarch eager for to greet her offspring, sculled the contents of her cup and pushed it into her husband's hand to sweep up her son in a whirling embrace.

'Mother, this is—' Simon was pushed eagerly away from his mother as Venus was greeted enthusiastically.

'Come, come, dear. You must be Venus. I am Lucinda, but you can call me Mum.' Lucinda pulled the newcomer towards the kitchen. 'We must get you away from these males.'

'How come I didn't know the fiancée's name in advance?' asked Alistair.

Lucinda shrugged. 'Did you care to ask the offspring sequenced at position two?'

Her husband shook his head negatively.

'Well then, that answers that. Is it not your mission to gather information for sorting our kith and kin into routines of normalcy?' The matriarch puffed out her chest, her generous bosom heaving in the curvy body.

'This is just too weird.' Venus pulled away from Simon's parents, inching backwards towards the frontal escape. 'I can't do this.'

Simon hurried towards his fiancée. 'What's wrong?'

'You are all trying too hard.' Venus's lower lip trembled, eyes widening as they continued their snail-paced retreat as if in hope of rescue.

'Nay, newcomer.' Uncle Bruce crushed the can in his hand. 'You are permeated with a personality to match a starched linen.'

Simon's cheeks were resplendent in scarlet reminiscent of humiliation, but his hands balled into fists as he replied in righteous outcry. 'This family unit is all mixed up. You defy the timeline somewhere between the regency era and the 1970s. No wonder my partner is of a bewildered constitution.'

'Quieten your speech, you are of an inferior age,' cried Grandpa Bruce.

'Halt ... I wonder.' Lucinda smiled disarmingly before reaching for a large broom and rushing towards Venus.

The wooden table was beclothed in a silver tablecloth and overladen with various bowls of cooked vegetation, sugary desserts and cardboard receptacles that made a loud crack when pulled by two beings as crepe paper crowns, playthings and papyrus with humorous etchings rewarded the players. The various beings hovered around the table, the device once emulating a broom had engulfed all in a green light before revealing the truth.

'We are so happy to have you here, newcomer.' Uncle Peter smiled and glubbed down another mouthful of his amber treasure.

'What is Venus like at this time of year?' asked Grandpa Bruce, the family unit's meteorologist.

The newcomer smiled. 'Hot as usual. This land down under feels like home.'

The blue-skinned fiancé squeezed her green webbed hand. 'Welcome home.'

The End

Hiss

I stretch, my whole-body flexing with unnatural elastic-ity, my muscles and sinews so in tune. I am the perfect gymnast, or so says my mum. I yawn as the digital alarm clock clacks over; Mum refuses to update the retro thing. I scowl in disgust. 3:01 am.

I pad softly across the bedroom floor, my mum and I share a one-bedroom apartment, it is all she can afford. I pull open the door, shoving my hand into the gap, it glides inwardly, silent like a ghost on a pre-emptive haunting.

Sighing, I swat apart the living room drapes, my eyes widening as the full moon comes into view, and a spiritual yearning rushes through me, as if this ancient satellite is a celestial being filling me with the urge to move my body in rhythmic worship.

Mum hates it when I feel the urge to scamper, cavorting across the ancient emerald carpet as if it is lush grass. My body pulses with the need to move. I step gracefully up onto the armrest of the monstrous leather couch that bears tears from my childhood. I was a biter, the chewy fabric cushioning sore gums from sharp teeth.

I pause for a moment, song rushing through me, vibrating from within as I tiptoe across the couch, humming some ancient lyrics, a tribute to my wild roots, the song of my people. My mother snorts from the other room. My ears prick up at the sound. I halt my gambolling, easing myself off the couch. I do not endeavour to incur Mum's wrath.

Rumble, gurgle, my stomach protests as starvation causes it to clench. In reflection, I haven't eaten in two hours. I rush towards the kitchenette, the living room a large, open-plan design. My caregiver has prepared a snack for me; she is a good mother, and so she should be, for I am her perfect child. I cram the biscuits into my mouth, chewing without decorum, wiping any residue with spittle applied to the back of a hand.

Starvation appeased, I toss a small ball from hand to hand, wiling away the prowling hours, contained in a shell of brick and wood, a dampener on my people's hunting instincts. *Hiss*. I jump, startled from my thoughts as the hideous noise envelops me. Shivering, I glance around, my lower lip trembling. Backing towards the couch, I scramble up upon it, as if it is a lifeboat in open water, protection from the sharks swarming below.

Hiss. The horrendous noise haunts me. I leap off the couch, scrambling haphazardly to the bedroom, calling out to my dear protector.

'Mum. Save me.'

My mum scrambles to a sitting position, her eyes opening and narrowing on me. 'Not again. You always do this.'

'I am terribly afflicted. A horrific sound threatens my ears and could be a danger to our safety.'

Mum sighs with resignation. 'Get to bed.'

I hang my head in appeasement as she points to my single bed, void of her comforting presence. She hasn't let me sleep in the huge bed since I vomited on her a few days ago. I was proud of that one, it was so big and furry. Like the dutiful daughter I am, I shuffle towards my bed as she lies back down, her mouth agape as the sound of rolling thunder escapes into the darkened room, her vibrations comforting, akin to my people.

I pause as the minutes clack by, my eyes affixed on the clock. The black, plastic leaves inscribed with white numbers flipping over as I bide my time.

I will hunt down the source of the noise. It is now 4:00 am. I hurry out of the room and grab a snack; I cannot help it. A loud noise of contentment falls from my lips. I scan the room, my eyes homed in on any possible movement. Any twitch or fall of shadow will capture my resolute stand.

Hiss. I duck down, stealthy in my pursuit of that insidious sound, the carpet bending ever so slightly under my weight as, on all fours, I make haste towards the couch. I dip my head, lowering my gaze between the wall and the back of the couch. A pair of red eyes blink. I gulp as the fell thing hisses yet again.

Enraged that the ancient enemy of my people dares to hunt me as if I am a ready meal my middle-aged mother heats up in the microwave. I scurry into the gap, howling with rage, spitting as I scrabble about. My opponent bites my hand. In revenge, I swipe at it with long nails.

'Begone pest, ancient foe.'

'Not before I devour a youngling of my bygone enemies.'

I roll my eyes. His people are of an ancient race. When the world fell to pestilence, my mother's people adopted my kin and blamed my adversary's people for their infliction. Tamed by gifts of a dairy nature, my people agreed to a contract: food and board, treats, affection, and to maintain our hygiene. In exchange, we would rid the world of the denizens that would harm the contracted.

'Why do you cling to the old ways with outdated speech and ideology?' I ask, inching closer as my foe scrambles against the wall, their eyes widening.

'My folk became crumpled leaves lost on the wind, dwindling as your people drove them from the towns.'

I shrug before I grin, baring sharpened canines. I pounce.

As I clean up, my mum storms out from the bedroom. With a click, light floods the room.

'Why are you hollering, Cleo?' she asks.

I puff out my chest, my gaze locked on my mum's. My foe vanquished; I smile triumphantly.

'Urrgh, not again. I will dispose of this before the land-lord comes poking his nose in again. Stay inside.' Mum unlatches the front door and hurries outside.

Chitter. Another ancient enemy. A newcomer has swept inside my abode through the open door. I lower myself down and scream my war cry. I must protect my mum like the princess and warrior I am. 'Meow. Just like that rat, death creeps towards you, cockroach.'

The End

The Intellectual

The surgery would take eight hours; I had little hope for his survival. Hell, I had little hope that any of us would survive. My hand trembles as sweat beads on my brow. I purse my lips, exhaling a hot breath through the blue mask covering my mouth, and raise the scalpel as the nurse wipes away sweat with a sterile cloth.

Licking my dry lips, I glance around the harsh, white-walled operating room. It is hot from the bright lights above the steel operating table draped with white, sanitised linen on which poor Mr Mersey lies under anaesthesia, awaiting the scalpel in hopes I can remove the tumour.

Blood wells up as I carefully press into the flesh, orange from the antiseptic applied to the skin. I have done this surgery hundreds of times now, my hands instinctively know what to do. Exhausted, I distract myself with thoughts of my patient and how I had met him six months ago. I had been in a sorry state. Like most people, I was in a perpetual state of fear. Media constantly bombarding us with stories of conflict, spreading disease, and people doing terrible things. Yikes. A hiss involuntary escapes my mouth. My neighbour had recently had her beloved cat stolen.

I had strolled around the neighbourhood, trying to find meaning in my life and had bumped into Mr Mersey, his nose in a book. He had chortled pleasantly, his cheeks rosy, his eyes clear and merry. I had sighed with resentment, for I disliked the incompetent at that time, and his book landed with a dull thud at my feet. My heart had long since hardened against compassion, my previous client, my beloved wife, passed away during surgery a year earlier. I was the attending surgeon.

I snatched up the book. An involuntary sigh escaped my mouth, blood seeping from the papercut on my thumb. I had nearly tossed the offending book at the elderly soul who gawked at me, his visage one of awe and genuine thankfulness.

'Thank you, kind sir,' stammered the man. 'That's a rare copy, a rare copy indeed.'

'No problem,' I had muttered.

'What's your name?' he had asked.

'Samuel.' I had flung it at him as I hurried past, wanting little contact with bothersome people.

Over the next few weeks, Mr Mersey had frequented the coffee shop where I got my morning expresso before heading to work across the road.

'Doctor. You must hurry,' the nurse mutters.

I glance at the clock, one hour already gone. My eyes settle on the incision, clean and perfect. I place the scalpel on the tray and lean in to gauge whether my guess had been well calculated.

'I will have to feel for it.' I gulp, my double-gloved hand reaching for the innards, my thoughts returning to Mr Mersey's previous and more lively engagements.

The kindly and intelligent gentlemen had shouted me a few cups of coffee on several occasions. One day, without asking, he plopped himself down at my lone table adrift in a sea of noisy conversation, the hissing of the coffee machine, laughter, and familiar and unfamiliar bodies all seated within the establishment, involved in the allotted ritual of luncheon.

I had scowled unkindly at him that day. But his friendly eyes had twinkled, his mouth turned up in a charming smile filled with a side of mirth.

'You are a very busy fellow and hard to track down.'

I had shrugged. 'Why does it matter?'

My new companion had tossed a book down on the table: *The Infliction of the Undead*. The name of the book had forced a scathing laugh from my mouth and I had glanced up at its owner. 'Why would I want to look at that?'

'I am Mr Mersey by the way. Just read it.' He stood, his chair squeaking, and he groaned as if standing was painful. 'You need to be aware of what's happening.'

I had rolled my eyes and shoved the book towards him. 'Are you nuts?'

He had smiled graciously, almost as if *I* was the strange person. 'Just read it.'

That book had hooked me, describing a new disease that had come from space. The cells had been used to try and cure tumours. I had laughed at first, but as I had continued reading and discussing that book with Mr Mersey in consecutive lunch breaks, I had realised he was an intelligent man. Especially when the news started reporting cases of an unknown disease which brought the dead back to life.

I tremble, exhaustion and sadness bringing me back to the present. I fumble around, feeling for the hard tumour.

'Excellent.' I grin at the nurse. 'I have it, I was right, I was right.'

Locked in the hospital and on auxiliary power, we couldn't rely on imaging as the radiologist had already succumbed to the pestilence.

I raise the scalpel and steel my shoulders. If I get this out he may survive. I caught it early enough, I hope.

Glancing at the clock, we're three hours in. A roar behind me causes me to turn. The door is pounded on from the other side. My eyes affix on the vibrant red splatters near the entryway.

The anaesthesiologist hurtles himself at the door, crashing his body against the chair jammed under the handles. 'Hurry, doc, you are the only one who can help him.'

The door splinters. A green, once human, hand covered in tumours resembling orange boils reaches for my best friend of many years and former researcher, Jacob. My friend screams as he is dragged through the gap, and I turn my attention back to my task, my heart thumping rapidly in my chest as a sense of numbness washes over me. Another loss.

'Who would have thought zombies were real?'

The question drags me from my thoughts, and I glance at the clock. I really need to hurry this up. 'Yeah, but good news, I am ready to close.'

'That is excellent, doctor.' The nurse rings her gloved hands together. 'How will we wake him?'

My stomach drops. 'Ah, yes.' I suture the wound shut as the nurse applies a dressing. 'Jacob told me a little about what to do with a slow anaesthesia and breathing tubes. I will slowly turn off the anaesthesia while you check his vitals. As his breathing slows down and regulates, we can remove the breathing tube and wait for him to wake up. I hope.'

The door groans behind me as I slowly turn off the medicine. A zombie lurches before us, snuffling as if searching for prey. I place a finger to my lips. The nurse nods as she glances at the vitals on the screen. I point to the breathing tube, the nurse slowly pulls it out as the zombie roars and staggers towards us.

I lift Mr Mersey's cumbersome body and charge around the side of the operating table, kicking the chair out from under the door handle. Nurse Sandra flings open the doors and tries to step aside. I barrel into her, forcing her into a run. We scramble past shambling bodies in various states of decay, enter the tiny staffroom equipped with small fridge, microwave, urn and table. As Sandra slams the door shut, I place Mr Mersey's body on the table.

Huffing, I lean over, heaving in copious amounts of air before I dump myself into a seat. Sandra frowns and lifts Mr Mersey's wrist to check his pulse as she glances at her watch.

'Steady.' She smiles. I nod as she places an ear to his chest. 'Breathing is good too.'

The kindly nurse fetches us a cup of coffee. As I blow on my scalding beverage, I chance a smile at her. Surely, she will remember soon.

'So, how do you know the patient?' she asks.

'I never knew my father. You see, he left me and my mother when I was born to pursue a career in science. My mother said he was brilliant, an intellectual.'

'Not too brilliant if he abandoned his kid.' Sandra leans over the table and pats my hand.

'How did we meet again?' she frowns.

I run a hand through her hair. 'You died on the operating table and Mr Mersey brought you back.'

'Mr Mersey, I know that name.' Her eyes widen. 'Isn't he an author?'

I nod. 'I've read his book, *The Infliction of the Undead.*'

Mr Mersey sits up suddenly with a groan, his eyes lock on Sandra's. 'You see, my dear, you are Mrs Sandra Dalage.'

Sandra laughs and warmth spreads throughout me. It's over a year since I heard her laugh.

'The doctor is Mr Dalage.' Sandra's lips tremble.

I pat my wife's hand. 'That's right, my dear, we are married. Mr Mersey is my estranged father and you are patient zero.'

The End

The Itch

There is nothing worse than an itch you cannot scratch. That sounds odd, I know, but this is my tale, and I tell you it's one hundred per cent true. And it all started with a speck of dust.

Last Thursday, there I was minding my own business, a cup of tea in my hand, as I drew back the curtain and surveyed the neighbourhood. It's a rather pleasant place, except for the folks at number four and thirteen. The weird lady at thirteen's garden is beastly, covered in wind chimes and creeping vines that block the view of her porch. Don't get me started on the scamps from number four; running across gardens, trampling flowers and laughing loudly as they kick a ball in the street.

My garden is my pride and joy, you see; neat rows of potted colour, a fabulous lawn and a freshly painted white picket fence that surrounds my gorgeous bungalow. Junior from across the road had just tossed a candy wrapper on the street as he went to check the mail. Being the environmentalist I am, I hailed him down and pleasantly requested he bin the offending rubbish. The child had the gall to cry and ran into his house shouting for his mother.

Well, the day went from mildly miserable to abhorrent in the space of a polite gesture and the wicked smile from an incorrigible stranger. I was minding my own business, watering my flowers, my eyes scanning the street, on the look out to smite injustice for all my fellow beings with moral character. It was a balmy day, early morning, the sun warm and the mild breeze scattering a floral scent as it brushed the tiny hairs on my forearms. I sighed with contentment, my knees creaking as I lowered myself, wincing as my lumbago played up. My nostrils flared as I bent over my flowers, inhaling their intoxicating scent.

'Hooroo.'

Craning my neck, my eyes narrowed as they settled on the stranger that dared interrupt me. Scowling, I rose, my middle-aged body complaining at the sudden onslaught of my rapid movement.

'What?' I asked my lips curling up in a smile.

The strangely dressed fellow grinned. 'My, my, that sneer is almost a smile. As if the mouth has forgotten to use those muscles with an expression that brings joy.'

I stared at the man, his speech and manner odd. Dressed in an over-sized trench coat, and a straw hat perched on his cranium. I glanced at his frilled shirt, copious amounts of blond curls rising out of the neckline like straw poking through a pillowcase when overstuffed. His stubble was the same colour as his chest hair, blond curls surrounded his skinny face, the rest hidden under the hat. His eyes twinkled with either merriment or glinted with evil; I shivered.

'Why did you say goodbye instead of hello?' I scratched my head.

The scruffy fellow winked. 'I am a topsy-turvy kind of guy.'

I rolled my eyes, a snort escaping my lips. 'They make them weird today.'

The stranger's eyes narrowed, and his lips pursed. 'Well, see here, that was very unkind to a jovial greeting.'

I shrugged. 'What is it you want? I don't want trouble from strangers.'

The fellow laughed gleefully, before his maw widened into a very strange grin, his eyes snapping to mine. I couldn't draw away. 'You know me well, Ms Nitch.'

I shivered involuntary. 'No, I have never met you before.'

The stranger tilted his hat, his hair falling over his face in a mass of sandy curls. Thunder cracked suddenly, the wind picked up as the shadows deepened, as if the sun had fled.

'Lies, lies, call the flies. Often you have stared and chortled with mirth at the garden of kindly Mrs Firth. Today the veil is so very fine, the creepy draws near, sending tingles down your spine. You dared belittle thirteen and four, you contentious old bore. An irritant amongst the kindly and lively, you are snively. I could add a word that rhymes with itch, but alas I will keep it PG. Today you will get a bargain, a lesson for free.'

Backing away, my lower lip trembled. 'Begone,' I managed to choke out.

The stranger clambered over the fence, his tattered, unlaced boots stepping cautiously over the flowers. He stalked towards me, his eyes like living coals, glowed cruelly amongst his curls like living embers tossed in a pile of hay,

'Ahhhhhh!' The scream rushed out of me. I scrunched up my eyes as his long spindly arms reached for me.

'Are you alright, Ms Nitch?' The familiar rasping voice caused my eyes to snap open, focusing in on Mrs Firth, the new age, self-proclaimed healer from number thirteen. I glanced at her tie-dyed dress, her long, red hair shambling down over long sleeves, crystals hanging on string around her neck, and her fingers adorned with rings. 'Yes.' I push out past my laden tongue. 'I don't need help from the weird.'

The younger woman sighed. 'Well, okay, have a blessed day.' She took a step forward before she turned back towards me. 'You seem to know what goes on around here. Someone has taken something very valuable from Ronnie.'

I laughed. 'No one cares about Ronnie.'

The woman had the audacity to weep and suddenly rush away. I shook myself with resolve and tossed my sandals aside as I pushed open the front door and slammed it behind me.

I startle awake, sweating profusely, the stranger's eyes burning behind my closed lids from a slowly fading nightmare. I open them and sit upright, glancing around as moonlight filters in from the window to the left of my bed. A burning sensation starts on the back of my right hand. I flick the switch on the lamp to the right of me nestled in the middle of the bedside table; warm yellow light reminiscent of cheddar floods the room. I study my hand, there is a small black speck as if a grain of soot had marked the dorsal side. I scratch at it absentmindedly. This simple act does nothing to relieve the itch.

I throw back the blanket and pad across the blue-carpeted floor to the bathroom, fitted out in yellow and brown tiles. Opening the faucet, I place my hand under the cooling lukewarm water. This action does nothing to subdue the itchiness. I scowl in the mirror and raise my hand for closer inspection, nothing has changed. I pull open the medicine cabinet, apply some bite ointment and wrap the hand in a bandage, then leave my bathroom, climb into bed and turn out the lamp.

Sleep evades me as my hand begins to burn, the irritation spreading. I should probably call the doctor. I glance at the alarm clock, it reads 11pm, closed. I am known to be stubborn—unobliging my mother always said—and refuse to admit defeat. The itchiness spreads. I rip off the bandage and gnaw at the offending speck like some half-starved predator gnawing on a collection of clean-picked bones. There is no redness, no sign of obvious irritation. I consider myself an intellectual and would be a laughingstock if I drove to the hospital and presented this hand for inspection.

Mrs Finch said she was a healer. No, I will not stoop so low as to ask for her help. I close my eyes and pinion my arms to the side, breathing deeply as my fingernails dig into my palms, itching to scratch the aggravated hand.

'Arrgh.' A cry issues from my lips as I bolt upright, throw back the blanket and stuff my feet into slippers. I grab my dressing gown as I pull open the front door. I try to hold myself with a sense of decorum, but the itch forces away any ounce of dignity I have left as I gnaw at my hand between bouts of incessant muttering. I know I look a fright.

Curtains are drawn back; the mother from number four pulls open a window. 'Are you alright, Ms Nitch?'

I am tempted to offer up a rude gesture, but my fingers are engaged in scratching the itch. 'Mind your business.'

My neighbour scowls, slams the window shut and draws the curtain closed. A streetlight flickers and goes out. My ears prickle as the sound of boots thud on the path behind me. I scamper forward as fast as my aging body can handle. The streetlight near me flickers out; the footsteps behind me quicken.

A low eerie whistle that lilts up into a familiar tune is carried on the wind as it picks up, swirling around me, tousling my grey hair. I halt, taking heaving breaths, and turn to face my would-be foe. The ebony depths of night greets me, harbouring the things that stalk the shadows and are whispered in warning in the primitive parts of the brain.

Eyes as red as coals float in the darkness just above my head as words are whispered in my ear. A touch on my shoulder; the familiar scent of hay makes my nostrils flare.

The scarecrow watches,
The scarecrow sees all.
He sees how the mighty did fall.
He doesn't creep, he doesn't pry.
He doesn't stand idly by.
He waits in the dark for the veil to thin,
Then he comes for kith and kin.
Those with a lesson to learn will cry for him to yield,
But he will administer their punishment before returning to his field.

I tremble, turn on my heel and run, scrambling in the dark. The wind picks up and loosens my gown's ties and I shrug it off. A sole porch light burns like a beacon, a saviour in a sea of darkness while a hungry shark chases me from behind. The whistling is taken up again as I pull open the gate and scramble up on to the deck of number thirteen and hammer on the door with clenched a fist, while gnawing at the itchy hand with my mouth.

The door is pulled open and Mabel Finch stares at me. 'You look a mess, Annie.'

'Something chases me.' I wheeze.

'You shouldn't be out on a night like tonight,' she mumbles and holds open the door as one of the many bells attached to windchimes on her porch begin to ring in the now blustery wind.

'Thank you.' I huff as I push past her.

She pulls the door closed. 'Follow me.'

Mabel walks down a small narrow hallway, still lit with gas lamps, her slippered feet gliding across the wooden surface like a spirit while my large feet creek with every footfall on the ancient, stained wood. I still know the way, though it's ten years since I last had tea here. We reach the living room—a chaotic space filled with tie-dyed shags, brightly coloured bean bags, and abstract and cubism art littered across the walls. He liked those too, that man a stain on our ancient friendship.

I fall into a bean bag. She brings me a cup of tea from the porcelain teapot and pushes it into my hands. I gulp greedily.

'What is it, Annie?' Her eyes soften.

'Something chased me singing that awful song you and him used to listen to on record ... when I caught you dancing in the lounge.'

'You never let me explain.' Mabel plops into a bean bag beside me and grips a hand, the itchy hand. I twist in her grip and the empty teacup plummets to the ground as I tear at the speck on my hand. 'You see, Annie, rumours start out like a speck and spread like a nasty irritant.' She smiles sadly. 'You listened to those rumours and became the thing you hate: a busybody. Then Ronnie went missing.'

There is a knock at the door.

'Excuse me.' My saviour stands and leaves to answer the door.

I scratch at that speck, my hand now torn and bleeding.

Thud, thud. Familiar footsteps. A whistle in that well known tune and that eerie voice. 'He doesn't stand idly by ...'

I rush to my feet and hurry into the kitchen, heading towards the back door, but I am not quick enough. A wiry but strong hand grips my shoulder and turns me towards them. A scratch of a record, then that old folk tune floods the space with music, and that familiar voice croons to me as I am swept up in a waltz and whisked into the living room. Mabel grins at me, her eyes narrowed on me and my former paramour.

'They never found him,' my former best friend croons. 'My dear Ronnie. In his memory I erected a scarecrow and poured enchantments on him every day for ten tears. Today his spirit was encapsulated in that form, the scarecrow you belittled everyday wearing his coat and hat.'

'You stole my beloved from me,' I cry. 'He was not without sin and I—'

Those eyes that burn like embers lock on my face and I glance up at my reincarnated paramour. 'Dealt with me.' He grins broadly and pulls me closer, leaning down he whispers in my ear. 'Those with a lesson to learn will cry for him to yield, but he will administer their punishment before returning to his field.'

'You always jumped to conclusions, my old friend,' Mabel calls out as we waltz faster and faster. Dizziness sweeps over me as I twirl in Ronnie's arms. 'You knew I was adopted. Ronnie was my half-brother.'

The itchiness spreads all over my body like a festering irritant I need to scratch, but my hands are caught up in Ronnie's. The prickly sensation encompasses my body, I glance down at my arms now made of straw.

'You will be a fine addition to my garden alongside my dear Ronnie. My brother will have his revenge, and this nice neighbourhood will be free of your interference.' Mabel's voice fades as my mouth fills with straw.

The End.

Scraps

The rowdy gaggle of adolescents conglomerated near the bain-maries; trays held out in offering for the subpar sustenance that would grace the plastic food delivery system. As usual, the bullies accosted their weaker peers. The popular girls applied lip gloss, smacking their lips before pouting and taking photos with their mobiles from various angles. Insults were hurled to foes which resulted in vulgar gestures being used in retaliation.

The next student pushed forward and pointed to the potato bake, one hundred scoops made the once firm and cheesy dish crumble into a white and lumpy mush. I scoop out the slop. With a plop, the lump makes contact with the white plate upon the tray. 'Juice or milk?' I ask the student.

'Juice,' answers Jace, one of the more respectful youths.

One hundred students to go and we have maybe five scoops of potato bake left, some luncheon meat and apples that have seen better days. 'Not much left,' I call out to a fellow lunch officer.

Rose mouths back, 'Shocking, isn't it?'

I nod and pick up a tray as a shield as the next student, a renowned troublemaker, tosses an open milk carton at me then upends Jace's tray. The principal, a penny pincher and strict enforcer of the rules, yells from across the room. 'Don, get over here.'

Don laughs and gesticulates to himself. 'I'll get out of this easy as Dad's on the finance board.'

Jace sighs and tries to clean up his mess. I toss him an apple. 'I'll deal with it later, kid.'

'Thanks, Mrs Kincade,' says Jace, absentmindedly scratching at an itch on his hand. 'Mozzie bite.'

I smile at the antics, the usual rowdiness for a Friday afternoon, and wave the child off before I grab the cleaning kit and exit from behind the serving area to clean up the mess. The children behind me begin to yell.

'What do you mean you only have apples left?'

'This sucks. Our parents pay for this poor excuse for a meal.'

'It isn't right.'

I sigh. *Looks like I will have to talk to the sour puss principle of Harmadge High.* This situation isn't right, and I need to do something about it. These kids deserve better than that muck we are forced to serve up. I dump the contents of my dustpan into the trash and hang up my apron.

'Madge, just going to talk to the principal.'

'Good luck,' Madge calls out. 'Reggie and I will wash up.'

'You give him a talking to for all of us,' Reggie pipes up.

I knock on the office door. A shadow rises from the other side and stalks towards the door, visible through the frosted pane of glass set in the door marked Principal Arustus. The door is pulled open and a bespectacled middle-aged man dressed in a navy suit smiles at me. 'Hello, please do come in, Mrs Kincade.'

I step past the small man and squash my generous build into the seat facing the large, foreboding desk. A tactic often used to scare students into submission as the authoritarian stares at them from behind the ominous desk.

The principal hurries and takes a seat, leaning down to peer at me. 'How can I help you?'

I sigh. 'This is the third time I have talked to you about the issue this month.'

Arustus's eyes narrow on mine. 'And this is the third time I've told you there isn't enough money to feed those children better. The parents already complain about the fifty cents monthly contribution. The government gives us one dollar a month subsidy and you expect the students to eat well on a dollar fifty a month?'

'Let me choose the recipes. There are two hundred students here, I can definitely produce a daily hot meal for them within that budget.' I give the principal and encouraging smile.

'Have you seen the prices of groceries?' Arustus peers over his spectacles. 'Hmmm?'

I nod. 'Yes, but I know how to shop frugally.'

The principal's lips set in a firm grim line and he stares absentmindedly at my red blouse. 'I will look in to it. You are dismissed.'

I grit my teeth to stop myself from loosing a curse word, and hurl myself to my feet, rush towards the door, open it and close it none too gently behind me. Then I loose a set of volatile words. 'Outrageous worm, ruffian, boot scraper.' Feeling relieved of my intense dislike for the fellow, I turn on my heel to return to the cafeteria and regale my colleagues of what had transpired.

The weekend passes. The usual mundane weekend of reading, grocery shopping and curling up on the couch with my cat Cleo since the passing of my husband last September. We were never blessed with children, so my Cleo is now my sole comfort. I enjoy the liveliness of my job, the laughter of children and their somewhat hilarious antics if not a bit too ostentatious. I arrive earlier and earlier to work these days to prep beforehand and hopefully engage in conversations with the other employees as they tell me about their bustling weekends filled with parties, beloveds or short getaways.

Swiping my timecard at the kitchen entrance, I glance back at the sky, streaked pink and orange as the sun slowly rises, the wind warm and warning me of the scorcher about to come. Shuffling inside, I close the door and enter the pantry to take and lay out the coffee sachets, tea bags, stirrers, sweeteners and tiny milk capsules ready for my colleagues. I yawn and switch on the urns, I assume they will want a cuppa this Monday morning.

As the urn boils, I fill a polystyrene cup with coffee, three spoonfuls of sugar, unmeasured of course and fill it to the brim with hot water and milk. Stirring the contents of my cup, I blow over it before taking a sip. My eyes rest on a large, yellow envelope in the middle of the food preparation bench with my name on it. I scull the contents of my cup and toss it into the bin, before tearing open the envelope.

My eyes travel across the surface of the official-looking document including the solicitor's logo and that of the high school.

Dear Mrs Kincade,

It is with unfortunate regret we have had to terminate the casual employees from kitchen service due to lack of government funding. We know this will come as a complete shock for you, but in fact it will make your work easier. We have done the following to lighten your workload.

Installed a dishwasher.

Have prepared all meals in large amounts which just need to be heated and served (defrost by leaving in the fridge the night prior to service). Provided disposable cutlery, plates and cups.

We look forward to your ongoing loyalty.

Regards,

Signed: Principal Arustus

Signed and witnessed by: P Macintre

My hands tremble as I am tempted to tear this atrocious letter into scraps. Slamming my hand into the bench, I wince; even more processed crap for those poor children. I swipe away the tears welling in my eyes, pull open the large freezer, gazing at the contents on the glass shelves. Large plastic bags, labelled in the principal's familiar penmanship and filled with saucy foods, catch my eyes: Bolognese, shepherd's pie, bean casserole.

I open the pantry, now filled with dehydrated vegetables, instant potatoes, dried beans, juice boxes and canned peas. I sigh, at least my spices seem untouched. Well, with this minimal amount of work, I will take it easy. Grabbing another cup of coffee, I wander into the staff room, plop down onto the couch, reach for the TV remote and begin clicking through the TV channels.

A movie, a game show and three coffees later, I have preheated the bain-maries and am back in the kitchen, having washed my hands and donned my hairnet and apron. After unhooking another large pot from above the stove, I place it on the element next to the other two, toss in some ground onion, garlic, salt and pepper and dump in the bean casserole. The smell is hard to describe, that common spell associated with canned and processed food, the pungent aroma of my spices, and the subtle undertones of canned tomatoes, beans and ketchup. All the meals had one thing in common, a tomato or saucy base. I am tempted to wipe my sweaty brow with the back of my hand, steam rising in the humid kitchen.

I shrug and let the saucepans bubble as I pour boiling hot water into a mixing bowl and whisk in the cheesy dehydrated potatoes to top the shepherd's pie mix. I glance at the mixtures; they are all thick and lumpy. I pull a masher out of a drawer and proceed to try and break down the long strands of mince. It takes a fair bit of effort before they are incorporated into the foul mix that has been deemed suitable for human consumption. I shrug. I've lost, what does it matter? I can't fight the system. This will be my last shift.

Gripping the stainless-steel trays, I plop the mixture into them, before topping the shepherd's pie with the potatoes and carry each one out to the bain-maries and place the covers on top to keep them warm. The lunch bell rings and the sound of excitable adolescents wooshes towards the double doors as they are thrust open. A group of hungry teens eager to eat their fill.

The children rush towards me, picking up their trays and holding them up as I place paper bowls of their choice on their tray along with a juice box.

'Are you alright, Mrs Kincade?' Jace asks.

I give him a smile and wave him on, he picks up a juice box and hurries away. The children down their meal with gusto before Principal Arustus gives a speech. 'There is plenty to go around.'

The children cheer, some even licking their bowls. 'I have a list of children each day who can go for seconds. You can thank Mrs Kincade. If it wasn't for her suggestion, I wouldn't have thought to outsource, letting the other staff go so you could all eat better on our meagre budget.'

'Boo.' Some of the well behaved students glare and shout at me.

Jace's mouth is agape, his eyes narrow on me as if I have betrayed him. Reggie is his older brother. After being in trouble for so long I had gotten him this job and he had kept out of trouble for months.

'Quiet,' the principal calls out. 'Now, I will read a list of today's recipients of seconds. First, Don Dusten.'

My heart thumps dully in my chest and I hurry back into the kitchen. The children blame me. I clutch at my chest, leaning against the refrigerator.

'You can't leave yet, Mrs Kincade.' The principal enters the kitchen, grinning at me, his eyes glinting with pride. 'You have children to serve.'

I glower, striding towards the horrid creep. 'I quit.'

He chuckles. 'Two weeks notice must be given, it's in your contract.'

'Arrgh.' I stalk out of the kitchen and begin serving the students coming back for seconds. After my shift, I pen a quick letter of resignation, giving my two weeks notice before heading home.

The final day, I am both saddened and gladdened. Jace no longer eats in the cafeteria, along with a large group of the well-behaved students. The main meal recipients seem to include bullies and rebellious students. I dish the slop into bowls with a revolting plop, the thick glop having become almost gelatinous, the meat content certainly higher than that of vegetables. The number of students is waning.

Don Dusten lets out a horrendous wail and clutches at his stomach. 'Owww.'

The principal hurries over, smiling as the art teacher frowns. 'It's that stomach bug going around.' The principal tilts his head in my direction. 'It's good she's quitting, maybe it's her unhygienic standards that are the cause of this.' He pats Don's back. 'Off to the nurse with you.'

I scowl in the principal's direction. 'Do not anger him. I need that last paycheque,' I mutter to myself.

After lunch is served, I run the pots though the dishwasher, empty the trash cans and set myself to cleaning, including sweeping and mopping. The last bell of the day has sounded, and I am reluctant to leave. I take the mop and bucket back to the storage closet, when I shiver as if a ghost is peeping out from the shadows, watching my every move.

Rip. Rip. Rip. A horrid sound. I put away the items I am carrying and, as stealthy as I can, walk towards the sound. It's coming from a small classroom; I peer through the window in the door. Seated at a desk is the principal, ripping up red fabric, the same colour on my blouse. Beside him, favoured Trudy, the head of the parent teacher committee, runs the fabric through a handheld grinder then tosses the scraps into a mixing bowl marked Bolognese.

'I'm a terribly good cook.' She giggles.

'And I am good at chopping vegetables,' The principal says.

I swallow hard, my eyes widening in disbelief. I push open the door and rush towards the evil doers like a battle-hardened soldier. 'You disgusting pair.'

'No one will believe you.' The principal chortles as my fist swings towards him.

Harmadge Times

Too hard to swallow; sabotaged meals served at Harmadge High.

Mrs Kincade, former cook at Hartmadge High, has been convicted of grounding down fabric found on sale to extend prepared meals. In an interview with the Principal, Mr Arustus, it was discovered since the resignation of her colleagues and the death of her husband, Mrs Kincade was acting strange. Principal Arustus said, "It is with regret I witnessed Mrs Kincade's metal health decline, including storming my office and, despite my reassurance we were working within out budget to feed the students, Mrs Kincade insisted she would sort the issue out herself."

The former cook insisted she had seen the principal and Trudy Everland, head of the parent teacher association, grounding down budget fabric to incorporate into meals. The fact that Mrs Kincade knew that the fabric used in sabotaging the meals was on sale, the same used in the blouse she had sewn and worn, was used in evidence against her and she was sentenced to two years in prison. Mrs Kincade maintains her innocence.

In additional news, incidents of bullying at the high school have dropped to an all-time low. Students who were inflicted with seconds at luncheon, have missed many days of school and upon returning have remained subdued.

The End

For a million bucks

I am destitute, there is no getting around that horrid fact. And if that isn't a kick in the rear when you are at rock bottom, it is raining, and I traded my umbrella for a stale sandwich. I glance back at my tattered grey case on wheels and hurry towards the meagre shelter of the bus stop. As I huddle against the back of the refuge, I pull my luggage closer, the little wheels leaving wet tracks like two serpents slithering next to each other in the downpour.

Rent was due two months ago and I couldn't afford to pay it. I haven't even given the landlord my two weeks notice. I know it's wrong, but I have fled with my tail between my legs, my pathetic case crammed full of my prized possessions, and legged it to the bus stop. I don't know where I'll go but the shops in this small town are closed on a Sunday, so maybe I'll just ride around on a day trip ticket for $4 and stay out of the rain.

I unzip the case and draw out a holey towel to dry my face and hair, grateful for that small commodity. If I was in a better situation, I would have ripped the towel up into scraps for my art. I rub the back of my neck as if a gentle touch from incorporeal fingers had ran their digits across my skin. My breath steams in the frigid air. I whip around, scanning the area for a threat. Glancing up, the overcast sky flickers with lightening; the sky darkening as twilight beckons.

A man walks towards the stop, dressed in a puffer jacket and jeans, and crams himself into the shelter, tramping the water from his sneakers and blowing on his hands. He stays far to the left, giving me as much space as he possibly can.

'The 634 should be along soon.' He offers up some small talk.

I groan inwardly, predetermining the next question. 'Terrible weather, isn't it? It's raining cats and dogs.'

I nod politely. 'Sure is.'

'You ok?' The guy glances down at my case. His eyes scan my hole-ridden shoes, rising up to glance at the air vents in my pants as I like to call them, to linger on the tattered sleeves of my jumper.

'I'm fine,' I blurt out.

'Clearly not.' The man reaches into his pocket and draws out his wallet, stepping out from the shelter to hail the bus. He climbs the steps and taps his bus card against the meter and takes a seat. Just for a moment I thought he would help me.

I scurry up behind and count out $4 into the driver's hand, who then hands me a ticket. 'A few weeks and we go all electric. No cash and no tickets.'

'Thanks for letting me know.' The bus is full, the only seat left is to the back of the vehicle, where two lanky teens have their feet on the large seat. They wink at me. Sighing, I grab hold of the overhanging arm loops and stand quietly, slowly defrosting in the humid vehicle, warmed with body heat. My nostrils flare as the rank smell of wet wool lingers after the doors slam shut, like a tomb.

I wobble on my feet as time passes too slowly, people begin exiting at various stops, leaving in huddles or as solo intrepid souls ready to brave the cold and wet. I glance at my cheap watch; 8pm. I squash myself into a vacant seat and close my eyes as fatigue washes over me.

My stomach gurgles loudly and I snap upright. Rubbing my bleary eyes, I stare at my watch. 10pm. Only the driver and I are left. Glancing out the window, the lonely sky is bereft of stars and moonlight. Sideways rain batters the large, foggy windows. The bus slows down near a stop; the streetlight allows me to notice the unfamiliar dirt road we are on.

A group of people wait silently. I press my face against the pane, peering at the cluster. They are oddly dressed, as if some are LARPers, some cosplayers, and the others historical reenactors. No two outfits are the same, but there is one strange similarity: a weird grin is affixed on their pale faces, a mix between a half-hearted smirk and a scowl. The doors open and the group enters the bus, shuffling up the stairs, their eyes blank of emotion. The lead person, a male in a trappiest suit, hands over a strange coin, the others follow suit; fifteen in total.

When they are seated, I step out of my seat and approach the driver. 'Excuse me, where are we?'

The driver looks in the mirror, the reflected eyes peering coldly into my soul. 'End of the road.'

'Wait, I will get off here then.' Not that I know where here is, but the way it was said was like it was a threat.

The driver presses a button in front of him, the doors slam shut. 'Can't allow that, not safe. Take your seat.'

'Let me off,' I cry.

The driver laughs. 'Oh no, my dear, you are the last and therefore our special guest. Don't worry, we will take care of you.' The bus begins to gather speed as if it had never stopped and I lurch backwards and fall into an empty seat.

One woman, dressed in a Victorian gown, flutters her lashes at me, that smile never changing. 'It will be okay, dearie.'

My heart clenches, the breath wooshes from my lungs as fear steals my consciousness.

I jolt awake as the bus slows, turning into a dreary road, it harkens towards an imposing mansion, at least two stories high. Large gates clang open unassisted; the bus slows to a crawl. Lights that resemble floating orbs light up the gravel driveway. The vehicle turns left past a small river to come to a halt in front of the building, the doors opening upon stopping.

The driver stands and stretches and removes his coat and badge to reveal an awful, ancient brown suit with coat tails, a white frilled shirt poking up from the evening jacket. 'We are here, folks. Ready for a lively evening of love?'

The passengers give an eerie collective nod, stand and begin shuffling towards the exit, that grin never wavering. The driver approaches me and holds out his hand. 'I'm Dave.'

I take a step back. 'Where am I?'

The driver smiles, that same unnerving grin, and reaches over me to the cargo hold and pulls down a large box and places it on the driver seat. 'Put it on and read the instructions. Then you can join us. If you don't want to, you are free to spend the night on the bus and I'll drive you back to town at dawn. But a hot meal and bed awaits you if you care to join us inside.'

My mouth drops open as the bus driver makes his statement before he turns on his heel and exits the vehicle. Sweat gathers on my brow and my eyes narrow on the box as I pull off the lid. A red hooded robe and gold mask shaped like a raven's beak awaits. I laugh at the ridiculousness and reach for the handwritten note, my eyes glancing at the scrawling, nearly illegible, writing.

Welcome honoured guest,

To the game show, For A Million Bucks. It seems you are down on your luck, alone and disheartened. Well, your life has taken an unexpected turn. You have a chance to find love and win a million smackeroos. No, I do not jest. Find love with one of our wealthy contestants before the cockerel crows six times and you will win up to the estimated value of a million dollars in prizes. If you agree, don this ancient garb and join us in the mansion. Ask for our host Dave ... oh and don't forget to seek answers if you have any questions.

Signed,
Lady Penfield.

I tremble with either delight or fear and take off my damp clothes, don the robe and mask and hurry down the steps, the letter in hand. The wind has died down to a dull roar and the rain has stopped. The group are nowhere to be seen as I approach Dave standing by the door.

I hand over the letter. 'This isn't real. Is this some kind of scheme? Do I have to buy shares? I have no money.'

Dave reaches into a pocket and pulls out a wad of cash and tosses it at me. A collection of fifty- and one-hundred-dollar notes scatter as I clutch at them, grabbing desperate fistfuls. 'That's for free. You can take that and still leave.'

'Nah, I want the million. What have I got to lose?' I grin at the man in front of me.

'That's up to interpretation.' Dave's eyes narrow on mine. 'Do you want to ask me anything?'

'When do we eat?' I ask.

'Soon, very soon.' Dave smirks and the front door opens, and I follow closely behind the bus driver.

I grip the armrest; butterflies dance unchecked in my stomach, sweat beads on my brow from the overhead fluorescent stage lights, and three cameras are aimed on the set where I am seated across from Dave in a large ancient, tacky armchair that smells faintly of mould. The cameras must be automatic because they seem to move unaided. The person I assume to be the director is issuing instructions to the small crowd of ten who are seated beyond the camera on simple bench seats. For a production offering me one million dollars as a prize, their set seems very frugal.

'Now, remember your expressions can't change, but for the sake of our viewers, to give those lonely folks hope, please follow these instructions. When the sign lights up red you say 'aww', when it's grey, it's a sharp gasp or 'ooh' depending on the scene. For blue, please clap, cheer or whistle, and when the sign is purple, give an enthusiastic 'boo'. No talking while we are filming please.' The audience nods in unison as the director issues instructions.

I have had a warm meal, turkey and gravy, mashed potatoes, and the amount I have eaten has made me feel sluggish. I yawn as the Director counts down until we are live.

'Twenty ... nineteen ...'

Dave leans forward. 'Remember, I will ask you the questions, all you have to do is answer.'

I nod and sit up, gripping the seat harder. 'Yep.'

'Twelve ... eleven.' calls the director.

'Any questions?' asks Dave.

'No.' I mutter.

'Three ... two ... one. We are live,' the director announces.

Out of nowhere, a haunting melody plays; its garish undertones remind me of all the icky things in the world:

burrowing worms, red eyes in the dark, insidious shadows of creepy things that disappear when the lights are turned on.

The audience begins to clap in tune with the song as the camera zooms in on Dave. 'Welcome, my dreary and lonely beings out there in TV land. We hope to warm the cockles of your non-beating hearts with true love on, *I… DATED … A … MORTAL.*' The music fades away and the other camera zooms in on me as Dave leans towards me. 'This is our special guest from the local village. The last passenger on the bus to hel—' Dave coughs. 'On their journey to true love.'

I wave shyly to the crowd like I had been instructed, having also been told I must not give out my name or any identifying information as it lessens some of the mystery around the show. The other two rules I must abide by, which seem strange, are: I must not leave my chair, and, I gulp, the final rule, I must plant a kiss on the last remaining love interest to win the money. 'Hey, I thought the show was called *For A Mill—*'

'Don't worry about that.' Dave gives me that strange grin and leans closer, inches from my face. 'Have you entered in this freely at a chance to win?'

'Yes,' I say hastily.

The host reclines in his chair and clasps his hands together. 'Well, love interest one has a keen enjoyment of exercise. Working as a former trapezist in a circus. Put your hands ... umm tentacles, digits etc, together for Mr Yunti; he likes slow walks at dusk. Don't we all?'

The crowd claps as, in a puff of cinematic smoke, the trapezist appears above us walking a tightrope. I crane my neck to watch, the special effects are what they must be saving their money for as there wasn't a tightrope above us before.

'Mr Yunti is brave, he never bothered with a safety net. He's all the more tender because of it?' announces Dave.

My eyes narrow on the host. 'Wha—'

'I ask all the questions here,' Dave growls, showing razor sharp canines. 'You had your chance.'

'But,' I mutter.

Dave hisses. 'Shush or I'll take a bite out of you.' The host composes himself and stands. 'Will Mr Yunti dive into your heart and make you fall for him like he fell all those years ago?'

I gasp as Yunti jumps and free falls, the crowd gasps and I squeeze my eyes shut. The crowd then cheers and whistles as I open one eye.

'Ta daa,' love interest number one cries out standing before us, he bows low.

'Do you think you could learn to cope with Mr Yunti's presence?' Dave smirks.

The crowd cries out, 'Oooh.' It undulates and reaches a crescendo before dropping away suddenly.

'Maybe,' I answer, my gaze fixated on Mr Yunti's pale face. His make-up is garish: yellow tinges under green eyes, his lower legs made to look bruised, his suit ripped in several areas leaving even darker contusions. I am usually a fan of horror or I wouldn't read strange anthologies, but this is just too real.

'It's a maybe,' Dave calls out.

The crowd cheers and whistles as Mr Yunti bows low and disappears. The set lights turn off; I am left clutching the armrest in complete darkness before a classical theme plays. A spotlight centres on the left part of the stage, the cameras turn and focus on a sole ballet dancer, her white pointe shoes look worn, her blue tutu is torn, there are gaping holes in her white tights and blue leotard. Despite her tatty ensemble, she dances gracefully, those striking eyes focus on my mask and she leaps towards me.

'Graceful, creative and with a love of the arts. Miss Celeste gave her all to her ballet, leaving her destitute to all but wither away. Because of that she enjoys large lengthy meals, especially a steak.' The host holds out a hand as the music stops; the ballerina clasps his hand. 'Will our contestant dance away with the lovely Miss Celeste to live in their own world, their happy ever after?' The stage lights come back on.

'Maybe,' I answer, my gaze fixed on Celeste, scrutinizing her face. Her face is a strange green, as is the rest of her physique from what I can see where her clothing is torn.

'Awww,' says the crowd.

Celeste disappears as Dave takes his seat. 'Our final love interest is of noble birth; she misses the simpler Victorian times and has graciously let us use her furnished mansion for the set of this, our final episode.'

'Final—' I startle as Dave leans forward to grip my arm.

'As you know, the fate of the world is always sealed with a kiss. Not one contestant has yet won the grand fortune for the evil side. They have either broken the rules or ... become the victim of a match gone wrong.' Dave grins as the crowd boos. 'Yes, that horrid daytime gameshow, *I loved an Angelic Being*, has always managed to set up perfect marriages and maintained the status quo.'

I need the money, I mentally repeat to myself, followed by, *This is just a TV show*. 'I ... I.'

The host leans over. 'You have made a choice?'

'Not ... Please, let me—' I gasp out

'No, we have one more love interest to interview.' The host looks past my shoulder to the right as the lady dressed in the Victorian ball gown glides on to the stage. 'Will the lovely Lady Penrith give her heart to the contestant when all those years ago she handed it away in trust and was forsaken, her broken heart taking the life force from her. Well?' Dave turns to me. 'Make a choice.'

'No,' I cry out.

'Boo,' yells the crowd.

'You agreed,' Dave growls.

The host stands and steps back, his chair shoved aside as the three contestants suddenly appear, their makeup and costumes peeling away. The ballerina, now ghoul, gnashes her teeth at me, the trapezist chatters with his skeletal jaw, and the Victorian heiress is translucent but where her heart should be is a gaping hole.

'Seal the fate of the world with a kiss. Before you become my next victim.' The vampire rushes towards me.

The three love interests step between me and the host, I catch my breath, touched by their protectiveness. What's the worst that could happen? I squeeze my eyes shut and pucker up.

I glance out the window, seated in my comfy armchair, another lovely day of mortal screams, fire and brimstone to look forward too. It's humid in the mansion, but at least the house and antique belongings remain whole. The wedding was done on set before the apocalypse, and I can't say I am unhappy. I blow on the cup of tea my lovely spouse made; they are very attentive.

My spouse's mouth is turned up in that strange grin I no longer fear and leans over to wipe my chin with a one-hundred-dollar bill. 'You are so cute when you forget to wipe your warm, squishy mortal face.'

Life is good, well for me anyway.

The End.

The buzzing started in the middle of the night, sending static pulsing along the fine hairs of my neck like a balloon rubbed on one's hair, causing them to stand to attention. I had just returned from the graveyard shift and I bet you, as the avid reader of my journalling, may assume I have returned from the night shift and a job commonly associated with this phrase such stacking shelves, a nurse or firefighter. No, I am a security officer for the local cemetery, and I work nights in a literal graveyard.

I toss my keys onto the bench near the copper kitchen sink and grab a tumbler from the overhead cupboard. Turning on the tap, I fill my cup and gulp down its contents before tossing it into the sink and opening the pantry to rummage around for some snack foods. Snatching up a half-eaten bag of chips, I cram them into my mouth to stave off the hunger before pulling open the freezer and taking out a frozen dinner and placing it in the microwave. Then I close the door and set it for two minutes. I stuff my headphones in my ears and connect them to my mobile and crank up the volume, drumming my fingers on the bench to a pop song and singing badly as I wait for my meal to finish cooking.

Buzz buzz, the whirring of wings,
While this lonely heart sings
My love flies to you,
On buzzing wings.

With the loud ding of the microwave, I grab a potholder and pull my spaghetti dinner out of the microwave. Peeling back the film, I grab a fork, twirling the spaghetti around the cutlery before shoving it into my mouth with a re-sounding smack of my lips before I continue to devour the contents. Tossing the black, empty tray in the trash can, I shrug off my suffocating jumper and outer jacket, scattering my clothes throughout the cluttered living room littered with soiled clothing, empty packets of biscuits and crisps, before shrugging out of my shoes, balling up my socks and flinging them on the couch. *I am a slovenly person and I love it.* I grin as I flump down onto the bed and reach for the item on the dresser. My heart quickens and I peel away the plastic, bring the CD cover up to my mouth and plant a kiss on one of the three men pictured on it. I draw back and sigh. I got this from a scalper in a dark alley at midday, paying a hefty price to get the limited edition, only three having ever been made.

I frown; that fellow had seemed familiar. As a hardcore member of The Flies fan club, I had entered every competition, and sent copious emails to the band. Then, one day I had been emailed by an unknown address telling me to meet with them to receive a free copy of a limited-edition CD. I had been duped and forced to hand over $500 to see if I was worthy enough of shedding materialistic chains to receive the item. He had even had the audacity to ask would I purchase it for a million bucks. I laugh. Hypocrisy at its finest. Opening up the CD player, I put the CD in and close the drawer. Track one begins to play.

I swipe a tear away with a thumb and sing, badly, in time to the song, *My Love Flies to You on Buzzing Wings.*

Buzz buzz, the whirring of wings,
While this lonely heart sings
My love flies to you,
On buzzing wings.

'Ah Rosco, my beloved crooner. My sweet popstar.' I mutter to myself. How could the entire band suddenly disappear a year ago?

With shaking hands, I open the CD cover and pluck out the songbook. A sachet falls on to the black bedspread. Clutching it, my eyes lock on the electric blue words scrawled above a glass of slime green liquid, *Fly With Me Juice.* I turn the packet over to read the instructions.

Come away with us, transform that vessel of heavy flesh, fly to us, love, on buzzing wings.

Slip the contents into one glass of water;
when the contents turn green, slurp it down
and wait for love to take wing on the rays
of the sun. Warning you cannot come back
from this. Only recommended for hardcore
fans.

I let out a whoop of joy, scramble up from my bed and
hurry to the kitchen, filling the glass in the sink before
dumping the sachet contents in and stirring with my finger
until it becomes green. Downing the contents, the thick-
ening liquid bubbles suddenly before oozing down my
throat. I cough, almost gagging on the bitter contents as
I wipe my mouth with the back of my hand.

I scramble across the living room into the bathroom
and peer at my reflection in the mirror, tapping my foot
impatiently before shrugging and leaving for the living
room to plop myself on the couch and begin scrolling
through my 'to be watched' list. My fingers tremble on the
remote as a show called *The Disappearance* pops up in my
recommended 'for you' list. Rosco's smiling face appears
on screen as I click on the suggestion, making my insides
clench and my heart flutter. 'My one true love, where are
you? I need closure.'

As I gawk at the screen, an incessant buzzing begins. I
grind my teeth as an insect buzzes near my ear. I try to swat

at the pest, my mother's words echoing in my mind: "If you don't clean up this mess no one will visit you and you will attract pests."

Rolling my eyes, I lie sideways on the couch, my body turned towards the TV, and kick out as the pest lands on my leg, my eyes widening as they alight on the largest blowfly I have ever seen. *Gross.* It lands on the couch rubbing its legs together nonchalantly, its red, creepy eyes affixed on mine as if it was engaging in pleasant conversation as it buzzes loudly.

I bend in the middle to reach a sitting position, reach for a dirty sock and slap at the annoying insect. It shoots towards the TV to land on Rosco's face as if mocking my dedication, our love. I pout, before sliding my feet on to the stained beige carpet and stand up. *Buzz.* My ears prickle as another of the creatures hovers around my head in a circular pattern as if mocking me, as if I don a make-believe crown like I am a sovereign of trash, my kingdom this messy abode and the flies my dedicated courtiers.

'Arrgh.' I utter a cry of frustration before waving my hands around to discourage the beast from its activity, its constant drones assaulting my ears. My CD player glitches, static pulses along my neck causing the tiny hairs to stand to attention as the CD player begins to buzz loudly. *What is going on?* The fly above my head flashes past me, the TV fly follows and I stumble over the jumbles of clothes in the room to stand in the doorway of my bedroom. My mouth hangs open as the insects buzz in time with the jammed CD before they turn their ruby, faceted eyes towards me. I slam my mouth shut, not wanting the foul pests to see my mouth as a potential habitat as I rush towards the CD player and unplug it. My hand shakes as I glance at it, now covered in coarse, wiry hair.

Bile rises in my throat as I rush out of the room, my lungs heaving, and scurry into the bathroom. I grab a razor and scrape it across my arm taking the elongated follicles with it. I glance up at my reflection and blink rapidly. My brows lift in shock as I peer through scarlet eyes. *I must be having a reaction to that drink.*

Bang, bang. I jump and exit the bathroom and hurry towards the front door and pull it open. The scalper stands there, his face set in that charming grin, those ruby eyes locked on mine. Rays of early morning light settle upon his black trench coat, his face almost completely hidden under the silver scarf wrapped around his neck and pulled up to cover his identity.

'What do you want?'

'To issue your prize.' He steps forwards as I back away. A fly leaves his shoulder, almost gracefully.

I gasp as I understand its lilting drones. 'While this lonely heart sings, my love flies to you on buzzing wings.'

The two insects behind me settle upon my shoulders, crooning the chorus. 'Come away with us, transform that vessel of heavy flesh, fly to us, love, on buzzing wings, and wait for love to take wing on the rays of the sun.'

'You see, my dear, I am a fly by night and man by day. I am also an experienced in-demand manager. My sorcery shot a certain band to instantaneous fame until one day they had to fulfill my bargain and become my courtiers. For I am the sovereign of insects.' The scalper grins and his nose and mouth fades away to reveal a proboscis before it reverts back as he advances on me.

'Leave, before I scream.' I scurry backwards, falling in a pile of refuse.

'Wonderful, smelly place you have here. You will make a great spouse.'

I shudder, my insides turning to jelly. 'Get out, you weirdo.'

A warm, deep voice whispers in my ear. 'Come with us, love. We will overthrow him one day and steal his immortality.'

Rosco's familiar voice soothes my fear and whispers of love that would outlast a lifetime.

'I will,' I mutter

The insect sovereign smiles before my body twitches and shrinks. My bare skin is now covered in coarse hair. A buzzing sound escapes my mouth, yet I understand its meaning. My wings twitch as the intruder scoops me up in to his hand. 'We will be happy.' He turns, withdraws a swatter from his jacket and slams it down on the three flies hovering nearby.

'No,' I buzz.

'I deal with traitors harshly,' cries my future spouse as he turns and leaves my former home.

The End.

Retreat

Your choices matter in this tale. Read the appropriate
subsection upon making your choice

That's it, you have had enough. You used to work a minimal wage job with a sixty-hour week and your boss was a stinker. The good news is you did something so unforgivable you won't be welcomed back.

You rev your motorcycle, your belongings stuffed in the pack on your back, your long hair streaming behind you, the rain driving in from all sides. The moon is full to bursting, lighting the sky up like some infallible nightlight, making the twinkling stars look like some cheap knock off. As the vehicle gathers speed, your heart beats rapidly, your body trembling with anticipation as you try to stay seated, despite the pouring rain, as the motorbike flies along.

You are making your way to a small town called Retreat, where you have purchased a caravan with the last of your savings in the hopes of living a more minimalistic life, free of stress and financial hardship. The rains slows into a fine mist as you zip past the sign that could easily be missed.

You reduce your speed to glance around, and note the presence of a café—that also masquerades as a post office—a cinema, a small general store, a hardware store, town hall, a few ramshackle houses and a police station. You rev the engine to startle a middle-aged fellow of small stature dressed in an ancient suit, sporting a monocle on his left eye.

'Well, I never. What a knave,' says the spooked fellow.

You wave as your vehicle rumbles past and pull up near the café. You kick out the stand and rev loudly to announce your presence. The gentleman hurries towards you, shaking his fist. You lift a leg over the bike and dismount stretching to your full and rather imposing figure. The little fellow in front of you brandishes his fist.

'You best be careful. The folk around here enjoy their peace and seclusion, and we don't want any trouble.'

Unfastening your helmet, you place it on the handles of the bike and remove the keys and pocket them before winking at the person in front of you. 'No problem. I'm looking for Arriar Fata, I am eager to start my new journey.'

The stranger raises a brow. 'I see. If I was you, I would get back on that atrocious motorised bicycle and leave. It isn't—' The man's slightly pointed ears twitch as the door to the café opens. Warm light and heat emanating from inside enticing to my tired and damp self.

'This bike is a 1923 Triumph H. It's a classic.' You glance back to the café as an elderly woman, bent in the middle, wearing an emerald dress with large pockets, shuffles over to us with the aid of a cane.

'Fare thee well,' the gentleman mutters as his eyes widen and his bottom lip quivers before he turns and scurries away.

The woman approaches and stares up at you before she gives a raspy laugh. 'Arthur Cloverbottom is a terribly stringent fellow. Works at the general store.' The woman winks at you. 'Well, I would be too if my clan went missing during the shifter riots of 1822.'

You tilt your head and glance her like a confused canine seeking answers from its master. 'Don't you mean 1922?'

She claps her hands together eagerly. 'That's the way they looked when we won.' She smiles, showing receding gums, yellowed and missing teeth. 'Sure, young one, that is surely what I meant. Memory isn't so great anymore.'

'Who is we?'

She waves away your protestations, clutches your hand and shoves a large brass key into your palm. 'I am Arriar Fata and this is the key to your new home.' Arriar pulls out a scroll of parchment from the pocket and unfurls it. 'Do you remember the email you read and signed upon purchase of the home?'

You nod. 'Yes.'

'Well, I shall reiterate the rules.' Clearing her throat, she continues in that raspy voice akin to sandpaper dragged across a stone. 'Rule number one, do not open the windows and doors on a starless night or when the moon is full.'

You roll your eyes, squashing down the laugh that tickles your insides.

'Do you want the deed?' She scowls.

'Sorry.' You give her an encouraging smile.

'Rule number two, never pick a four-leaf clover from outside the boundaries of the town. Number three, do not leave out milk. Rule four, and the most important, if you hear unsolicited music in a language you don't understand, do not investigate.' Folding up the scroll, she gives me a cunning smile before holding it out to me. 'Do you agree?'

You sigh, eager to get this odd interaction over with. 'Yeah.' I take the protruding article before I wave.

'Well, take care.'

'How do I get to the place?' You ask.

'Follow the main road north for twenty minutes until you see a ruin on the right. There will be a dirt track, follow that through Tarmnar woods until you reach the clearing and the end of the road.' She gives me a sly smile.

You suppress the shiver crawling up from deep within and gulp.

'Do you want to ask a question?' She stares at me, awaiting my answer.

You must make a choice. If you ask a question read section one if not proceed to section two.

SECTION ONE

'Don't follow any strange noises.'

You roll your eyes. 'Okay.'

Reaching into her pocket, Arriar hands you a small pouch. You open the bag and take a whiff, nostrils flaring at the salty smell. Reaching out, you touch the granules. 'Sea salt?'

'When you hear lyrics sung in a strange language stand in a circle of salt and do not leave until the song ends. This is very important. If you hear an animal or something scratching at your door, do not investigate.'

You pocket the pouch of salt.

On to section two.

SECTION TWO

'Ah, thanks, and see you around,' You mutter.

'She turns and hoists her hand in a quick wave before shuffling back inside and closing the door.

The light is extinguished, and the night has become a lot colder. You glance up at the inky sky free of stars, fear pulsating through you like an adventurer holding an spluttering candle in a room full of monsters creeping towards them.

'Stop it, you fool. You do not have the gift of insight like your mother.' Shouldering off the pack, you unzip it and push the scroll inside and close it before shoving the house key in your pocket. You don the helmet, and start the vehicle by thrusting your foot down on the kick start. Walking the bike a few steps forward releases it from the centre stand. As the engine roars to life, you jump on, reach down and release another lever before pulling away from the curb.

You find the turn. Entering the road, the bike is suddenly tossed about like some canoe caught in rapids. Your whole body vibrates as the wheels try to keep their purchase on the washboard surface of the poor-quality road. You slow the bike; weariness washes over you. As the road ends sharply, you enter the dark, dank, almost silent woods, the headlamp barely making a dent in the pitch black. The outlines of the ancient trees, bending under their enormous boughs, look like ancient giants, heads bowed, their spindly limbs like jagged claws ready to capture unwary souls.

The light flickers and the crickets stop chirping as the hair on the back of your neck prickles.

Choice: If you choose to rely on the intuition inherited by your mother read on. If you do not, please proceed to section three.

You stop and hold your breath as your heart pounds in your chest. The light flickers again and you see a shadow crouching a few feet from the headlamp. Your gaze collides with those red eyes as a canine snout opens, revealing yellowed fangs. Another larger wolf steps into the light. You would have hit one only to be attacked by its friend, your gift has saved you. You rev your engine and shout. The noise startles your would-be foes and they scatter, dispersing into the darkness as if they were ethereal beasts.

Proceed to section four.

Section Three

You ignore your intuition and proceed onward. Thud. You collide with some obstacle in the dark and are thrown from your bike. Grr. Your breath catches in your lungs and you wince as you glance down at your leg, the material of your pants shredded. You touch the spot; your hand comes away hot and sticky while your nostrils flare at the scent of blood.

An awful howl forces you to turn your head as a large black wolf steps out of the shadows.

If you asked questions in section one, you retrieve the pouch of sea salt and make a rough circle around you. The unnaturally large wolf snaps its jaws as it paces back and forth, before eventually padding away into the darkness, as it were merely an ethereal beast and not some physical manifestation.

You shoulder off your pack. Unzipping it, you pull out the first aid kit, clean the wound and apply a dressing before trying to stand. You pull your bike back up and walk it around the wolf body before you get astride your trusty bike, proceeding cautiously down the path and on to section four.

If you didn't ask any questions, the beast pads over to you. Scrambling away, you drag yourself through the dirt, your injured leg causing you to wince. The wolf lowers its open maw. Hot breath tainted with the scent of lingering carrion washes over you and you pinch your nose in an attempt to repel the stink. Its teeth graze your neck before you close your eyes. The beast your doom.

The End

Section Four

You notice the clearing and slow your bike. A large rusty caravan takes up most of the space. An oil lantern hangs upon a pole, swaying in the cold breeze, its cheery flickering flame a welcome sight. You pop out the centre stand, turn off the engine and retrieve the brass key from your pocket. Trudging up the path, you pull open the screen door, put the key in the lock and turn it. The front door squeaks open and you feel around for a switch.

Click. Welcoming light floods the van. You scan the area. A large bed near a window to the left of you, a small kitchenette to the right near another window. You walk six feet forward to a sliding door, pulling it open to reveal a small bathroom equipped with a composting toilet, shower, sink, wardrobe and washer. You look out the back window. A shadowy outline of a water tank catches your eyes before you turn and wash your face. Opening the wardrobe, you pull out of your pack a few changes of clothes, towels toiletries and the first aid kit, and manoeuvre them into the space. Shoving the door shut, you exit the bathroom and slide the bathroom door closed.

Withdrawing the sleeping bag from the pack, you toss the empty bag onto the floor and flop down on the bed, pull the bag over you and fall asleep. Wake up in **section five.**

SECTION FIVE

You toss restlessly in your sleep, the cold seeping into your bones. A distant scratching pulls you unwillingly from your sleep. Pushing the sleeping bag to one side, you sit up. Your hazy mind tries to recall some advice, like it is long since forgotten. As the bone jarring howls of wolves nearby make you shiver, the well-meaning words slip further away as the baying of the wolves tempts you to leave the confines of your home and begin investigating the scratching.

Choice: Do you investigate the scratching and disregard Arriar's advice? If so proceed to section six. If you remember her advice, continue reading.

You remember Arriar's advice and lie back down, leaving the predators of the woods to contend with each other's company. The rest of the night is uneventful, and you awake to the sound of birds chirping happily as sunlight streams through the window. You make use of the facilities before opening the refrigerator and checking the contents of the overhead cupboards. You smile to yourself, noting you have about a week's supplies of food and, more importantly, a month of coffee. Preparing yourself a cup, you drink it straight without sugar or preferred milk, like the brave rebel you are, its hot liquid warming your insides and fortifying your resolve and washing away last night's fears.

Grabbing a bottle of water and a few snacks, you spend the day checking out the surrounding areas before coming back for a leisurely dinner. The sun drops below the horizon, the night is clear and the stars twinkle merrily as you drag a chair out under the caravan awning, sipping a cup of your favourite soup. As the night deepens, your head lowers as your lids droop. The refrains of a sweet melody in an ancient language you can't understand makes you lift your head and open your eyes. You raise your brows, your mouth opening wide as a being of pure light twirls past caught up in a rapturous dance. Their beaming smile and lilting words make your body twitch with the urge to follow.

Choice: Do you take the last of the salt and make yourself a circle or follow the fae-like being? If you are caught up in the dance, prance joyously on to section seven. If you use the salt, read on.

You surround yourself with a circle of salt, the being smiles sadly before she disappears into the night. You wait for a few moments before you rush inside. Proceed with haste to section eight.

Section Six

Standing, you hurry to the door. Pulling it open, you step outside and glance up. Sitting upon the roof's solar panels is a strange hybrid. They appear comfortable, reclining leisurely, their fur-covered, bipedal legs crossed over each other. Your gaze travels up their form; from a hairy torso and two hairless arms to a face with human eyes, ears and wolfish muzzle. The creature pants; its wolfish maw opens further as its gravelly voice makes your breath catch in your throat.

'Will you invite me to dinner?' The werewolf tilts its head as if awaiting your answer.

A scream gurgles up your throat and claws its way out your mouth, echoing in the woods. You turn on your heel and run towards your vehicle. The beast leaps upon you, its jaws snapping near your ear before it latches onto your arm. It pulls away, releasing your appendage. You gaze down in horror at the large bite. You crane your neck and watch the were-creature change shape, taking the form of a large wolf.

'Follow, pup,' it growls.

Pain envelops your body and you lie down. As you writhe on the ground, your body changes into that of a humanoid hybrid, not human and not quite wolf. 'No,' you mutter.

'Be at ease, pup. You will be able to take full wolf form soon enough. Now, do not dally, we must join the hunt.' The wolf bounds away.

You follow, your feet pounding the earth as you howl, your voice is soon accompanied by that of your new pack.

The End.

SECTION SEVEN

Your body is caught up in the unearthly music, it twists and turns of its own accord as you are enveloped in the joyous dance. You pass deeper into the woods. Time slows and you are almost unaware as the sun rises and sets many times, the trees growing, flowers drooping and decaying before springing anew. You sprout a set of wings, dazzling yet broken as if grief had poked holes in them as the years passed. Thoughts of your friends and loved ones passing as time churns on causes tears to form and spill down your cheeks until you pass into a glade that is so mesmerising you crumble to your knees as the song finishes.

The fae kneels before you and touches a hand to your cheek. Their touch is electrifying, sending a jolt through your body, awakening your soul as lost memories flood through you. You are a fairy, a lost member of the fae. The being in front of you is your beloved. They offer you a hand and you press your own into theirs as they help you stand. As the sun rises above the glade, you notice many creatures believed to be myth. A unicorn whinnies and tosses their mane before kicking up their hooves and thundering past. A group of fairies hover above flowers collecting pollen or nattering amongst themselves while seated on a circular cluster of toadstools sipping steaming liquid from petal cups. The smell of sweet tea causes your mouth to water.

'Your wings were pierced by the grief you suffered in our time apart.' Your beloved caresses your cheek.

'How did I forget?' you ask.

'You were cursed during the war by a vengeful fae.' Your beloved smiles. 'But all is well now that you are here. If we end the curse, your wings will heal.'

'How do I break this curse?'

My beloved leans forwards and places a chaste kiss on my lips and pulls away. 'It is done.'

Joy floods my body, and I give over to prancing and whirling with my dear one as a pan begins to play a lively tune on their pipes. I am happy knowing I am where I am meant to be.

The End.

SECTION EIGHT

Rushing inside, you cram your belongings into your backpack, snatch up your helmet and hurry outside. Striding to your bike, you shoulder your pack, straddle the vehicle and start it. The engine roars to life, as you pull away slowly gathering speed, a sense of relief washes over you as you leave the woods and head back to town.

When you arrive, you pull up, leave the vehicle and hurry to the café. Tugging open the door, you spot Arriar dozing in a cozy chair near a low-banked fire. She grunts before opening her eyes to stare at you.

'What is it? You look like you have seen your doom.'

You pull the parchment from your pack and place it on her lap before tossing her the key. 'I have a forty-eight-hour cooling off period after accepting the key. I'll await my refund.'

She cackles suddenly and you clench your fists together, that sound piercing through you. 'That is fine, my lively one.' Her mouth turns up in a wicked smile before she pulls up the sleeve on her shirt. You notice the arm is covered in bandages. She begins to unravel the binds; untwining it until there is a large pile on the floor resembling unravelled toilet paper.

Arriar leans forward in her chair, her eyes burn like hot coals. She lays the key on her papery flesh before beginning to rebind the arm. You back away in retreat like some frightened animal. You nearly trip over the doorstep as you turn and hurry down the street. You reach the bike and climb aboard, before pulling away from the curb. Gathering speed, you are soon on the open road heading towards the city. Hopefully your boss can forgive you for toilet papering their house and you can get your old job back. At least you are alive.

The End.

Malodorous

I cover my nose and mouth with my palm, my stomach churning as I force back down the bile. Rushing towards the closed door, I take an unfortunate breath as a I struggle with the handle, trying to pull open the large steel doors. Hurrying outside, I give up any pretence at decorum, gifting the curb the contents of my dinner.

Gasping for breath, I am bent double as my stomach clenches, threatening another bout of upheaval. What was that smell? Can I even describe the awfulness as it crawled up my nostrils like some foul thing looking for a darkened retreat to conceal itself from prying eyes.

This has to be the worst job I have ever been called out to as a plumber, and I am not sure I can finish it despite the hefty paycheque. I fix my overalls before hurrying over to the van and retrieving an odour mask. Donning the protective wear, I compose myself, before hurrying back towards the doors of the desalination plant. I have been tasked with finding and repairing the leaking pipes for the staff amenities. The normal employees have left for the day, leaving a skeleton crew, on for basic operations, and a few security guards scattered about the site.

I pull open the doors and enter the white-walled hallway. Lights attached to the cement wall hum with electricity and give off a sickly yellow light. My work boots thud dully on the matching floor. I come to the end of the passage and take the left. Ascending two flights of stairs, I take a corridor to the right before descending another flight of stairs and entering the staff bathrooms from which the foul smell had arisen. I set to work, plunging the loos before flushing them.

I pull up my mask and gasp, that horrendous smell not as powerful, still lingers. I thrust my mask back over the lower part of my face. An employee enters the facilities and coughs before covering their mouth and mumbling, 'What is that smell?'

Shrugging, I reply, my voice muffled under the mask. 'Trying to find the cause of it.'

'I'm cleaning staff, I'll remove the trash.' They don a pair of gloves and remove the trash bags, replacing them before leaving the room with the full ones.

I reach for a can of deodorizer on a shelf stocked with hand wash and toilet paper, and spray each cubicle before removing my gloves, tossing them in the trash and washing my hands thoroughly. I cautiously take off my mask. Faint traces of that horrible scent remain, but it is tolerable. The staff member returns with a cleaning trolley and gestures for me to leave. Following through with their wishes, I retrieve my gear and follow the wall, descending down five sets of steps, and follow the directions laid out on the map I have pulled from my pocket.

Highlighted on the map is the area marked pipe room, and I gaze down over the railing. My mouth drops open in amazement. Large pipes of various descriptors run along the walls and floors; an occasional hiss denotes most are busy fulfilling their purpose. A large machine built in the centre hums with power. I hurry down the last set of steps, feeling that power vibrate through my being as my boots touch that final floor. That power, that purpose, makes me almost drool.

I love my job and how vital I am for the contingency of mainstream life. I reach out and run my fingers along the smaller grey pipes labelled sewage; it is cold to the touch. I remove my mask; beads of perspiration appear on my brow in the humid space. A huge hiss makes me jump and I laugh out loud. I wriggle my nose as that familiar scent wafts out from a darkened passageway, barely bigger than a crawl space. I pull out a torch from my toolbelt and glance at the words painted on the wall in large, green letters: *sewer access.*

Click. Turning on my torch, I hold it up and peer into the tight space, barely four feet across. The pipes running along the left wall barely leave enough space between the place they are attached and the opposing wall. A wave of unnecessary fear washes over me and I shake myself briefly, trying to rid myself of it. I have heard rumours that a woman from a group tour wandered off and became trapped in one of the many corridors never to be seen again.

I enter the passageway, my torch barely making a dent in the humid dark. I will have to complain to management about how dangerous this is for staff. As I move forward, the box cutter on my belt scrapes along the wall. It dislodges and plummets into the dark with a clunk as it hits solid ground. I angle my torch and begin searching for the lost tool.

Squelch. Hiss. I startle at the strange noises and glance around. A glint in the dark and I bend down to retrieve my tool. Shifting my plunger to the other hand, I grip it in the hand my torch occupies before stepping forward. I count my steps, concentrating the beam of light on the pipes, looking for cracks or leaks. Two hundred steps in and none to be found.

Scritch, scratch. I pause trying to determine the source of the noise, maybe a rodent scurrying past. Another hundred feet. *Squish, squelch.* I need to find that ominous noise. Two hundred feet further I remove my mask, almost gagging at the smell. Rot, sewerage, all mingled together, blended with the suffocating heat and oppressive dark, causes sweat to run down the back of my neck. I drop the plunger and my mask as I gag. Retrieving my mask,

I hastily place it back on and aim the beam of light from my torch at the source of the smell. *Squelch, plop, squelch squish.* A thick, green ooze bubbles out of a large crack in the PVC piping and plops onto the floor.

The pipe will have to be removed at a later date, but for now I don a pair of gloves and reach for the trusty self-fusing silicone tape strapped to my work belt. Something rustles nearby and I turn my head to stare into the darkness.

'F … ree … me.' It is an almost inaudible whisper.

'What the heck is that?' Trembling, I place the torch on a lower pipe and aim the light towards the crack. I need to finish the job, for the rent won't pay itself. I know this will be a rush job, but I need to get out of here and into sunlight and fresh air. Heck, I'll take a quarter of what's offered; I won't be coming back.

I begin winding the tape around the break until it no longer leaks. The squelching noise slowly fades away and I sigh with relief. *Scritch, scritch.* The sound is like elongated fingernails trying to claw through thick plastic. Shuddering, I take a step back, leaning against the opposite wall trying to gather my thoughts.

Striding forward, I begin tapping on the pipe around the newly fixed area; something gurgles like someone taking a last breath under water. That's it, I'm done. I lean down, reaching for my torch. A ripping noise causes me to glance up. Long, black strands of hair covered in that foul oozing substance dangle down and brush against my face.

'F ... ree ... me.'

'No.'

'You must!' The tape is torn away as the elongated claws rip it to shreds, and a bony hand points at me. 'I need atonement.'

A scream claws its way up my throat and out my mouth as I turn and hurtle back the way I came. *Scritch, scritch*. Nails on plastic as the undead creature scrambles along the inside of the pipes, trying to follow me. That malodorous scent wafts on the humid air and I toss away the suffocating mask only to gag. My boots thud on the cement, light appears at the end of the passageway, but a rustle to my side makes me shine my light on the pipes. A ghoul, leathery skin stretched taut; that black hair bedraggled and covered in grime. Its mouth curls up in an unholy grin as it launches itself at me.

I brandish the box cutter like some holy talisman. It moans and backs off, hissing.

'Atonement,' it wails.

I stutter in response as my heart hammers in my chest. A sole tear rolls down my cheek. 'It was ... an accident ... Maran.'

'Liar.' My undead ex hurls itself at me. 'You did this to me.'

Maran grabs me by the scruff of the neck, dragging me into the pipe with supernatural strength. 'You promised me love and marriage.'

My voice is drowned as that foul ooze washes over us, my nails digging into the PVC. *Scritch, scritch*. At least we will be together, and no one will know how we fought on that job interview tour or how we became lost. They will never find out that she slipped and fell when I left her in the dark passageway. And surely it cannot be discerned how, when I returned and saw her unconscious, I panicked and widened a small crack in the pipe and laid my princess to rest in a tomb of grime. My body, then wracked with fear and guilt, caused me to flee, the hissing of the pipes her supposed final goodbye as her body was swept away from the light.

How was I to know they would hire me days later and ask me to repair the leak I worsened. Hopefully they will never figure it out.

'Together at last,' she whispers in my ear as we float down that grimy tunnel of love together, her arms wrapped around me.

The End.

Silver Bells

My mother was an unusual person and named me after her favourite English nursery rhyme. She was also an avid gardener and favoured the marigold. Hence, here I am, Mary Cockleshell, staring at those detestable flowers all neatly lined up in a row. My mother passed away a month ago and I have inherited her little shack near the beach. I stare at the ramshackle rusty gate, the keys clutched in my hand.

I gaze at the overflowing malodorous bin situated behind the fence, harbouring weeks of unemptied trash. The gate squeaks relentlessly as I shove it open, before gripping the handle of the wheelie bin and hauling down the mildly sloped driveway to the dirt road. It thumps in protest as I let go. It rocks slightly before it settles on its base. One task done. At least it will be emptied this morning. A monthly service. It will soon be full again when I deep clean the house.

I dawdle up the driveway, avoiding the strange spectacle that is my mother's garden. A row of marigold, and a line of common silverbells. The appearance of the silvery white flowers almost appearing upside down like a cluster of bells synonymous with the plant's name. This sight would almost be beautiful if it wasn't for the oddity of the circular low wall surrounding the flowers made of white marble and encrusted with cockle shells.

A large, bell made of silver set atop a wooden pole stands in the centre of the garden. A white, corded string dangles down. I wipe a tear away, suddenly remembering happier days as a small child, snuggled in my mother's arms as she danced around the garden whispering obscure words before kneeling before the pole. Unleashing a dazzling smile, she had pointed to the cord and nodded at me. Rushing forward, I had rang that bell with wild abandon as if completing some forbidden ritual.

My eyes swim with tears. As if drawn by some unseen force, I hurry towards the bell, my hand reaching for the cord as the bell tolls one last time for the beloved dead. The wind whips up, fragrant with hints of flowery undertones and the salty spray of the ocean. I turn and glance to the right, the sand from the beach coming up to meet the fenced off driveway. The waves churn relentlessly like my grief, my pain a grinding mess of bitterness at my estrangement from my mother this past year and twinges of love for the fond memories I have of her from my childhood.

Taking one last glance at the garden, I hasten towards the front door, unlock it and step inside. I sneeze, the dust particles dancing in the sunlight streaming down from the skylight. I could imagine my mother's whimsical tales at play here, little fairies dancing on the rays of sunlight for the sole purpose of making a child laugh.

Trudging down the hallway, my grief lies heavily on my mind, like someone sitting upon my shoulders as I clamber up a steep incline. I halt outside my mother's bedroom, afraid to open the door in case her restless spirit hovers on the other side. I shake myself, my mouth curling up into a smirk as I almost laugh at the ridiculousness of such a thought.

Turning the handle, and with a gentle push, the door glides silently over the dark, stained wooden floor. I flick a switch. Light floods the room as I scan the space, taking in the bright yellow curtains, four poster bed with purple drapes and the fluffy rug on the floor Mother and I tie-dyed when I was eight. The back wall has an antique vanity and giant oak bookshelves lined with books on astrology, numerology, myths and legends, and other eclectic books including a dusty tome I was forbidden to read.

I reach for the tome. My stomach drops and the room chills rapidly. A bell chimes, and I whip around as the light goes out with a sudden crackle of electricity. Blue light sparks and illuminates a figure crouched on the floor. My mouth drops open and I back into the bookcase, stumbling against the comforting firmness, my hands scrabbling at the shelves to guide my body as I slide to the floor. The electricity sparks one more time before the figure stands and approaches me, their face covered in black streaks, their mousy brown hair frizzled. My eyes scan their outfit, a coarse linen shirt, full-skirted knee length coat that had seen better days, hose, rough spun knee breeches, and a pair of well-worn shoes. Their piercing blue eyes lock on mine. Their stare seems hungry for something I can't fathom, as if filled with grief and undertones of relief. They appear to be around thirty, a few years my senior.

Glancing towards the door, I leap to my feet and hurtle across the bedroom. My sneakered feet squeak as I am dragged into the man's arms. His eyes linger on my mouth before he presses several kisses to my cheeks. His own flush as he pulls away, his hand on my shoulder to steady me.

Bowing low, he draws himself to his fall height, a good foot taller than myself, and he flashes me a charming grin. 'Well, if I haven't found my own dear Mary. You rang for your beloved?'

'What ... What is going on?' I splutter.

The intruder glances around. 'Right, you have forgotten. Your ma said you would have.'

I blink rapidly. 'Are you some historical reenactor or maybe a stage magician?'

The man chortles. 'No, I am William and you are a witch like your ma before you. My own vocation is that of warlock, and you happen to be my betrothed.' He smiles and waves his hands over my head. 'You are exhausted from grief. You will need rest before he comes for you.'

I feel myself falling as I faint.

My nostrils flare as the smell of soup reaches them, interlaced with the smell of wax and burning candles. I blink rapidly, trying to focus. I am in my mother's bed where she died. I scramble upright. William has retrieved the candles my mother kept in the living room and lit them. He sits in the middle of the floor with a lit candle. A wooden bowl is held over it, and steam rises above the bowl as the scent of tomato soup makes my mouth water. How does his hand not burn?

He is distracted, so I slip out from under the covers and pad towards the door. The floor creaks and I halt.

'Those metal things you keep soup in are ridiculous to open. I tried with force and then a knife. The thing did not open so I resorted to magic.'

I swivel about face. We lock eyes. A jolt flows through me and my heart begins hammering in my chest. 'Why are you in my house?'

William shrugs. 'I have already told you some of it.'

'That is a fanciful tale.'

He shakes his head and takes a step towards me. 'Your ma said tomato broth was your favourite.'

'How do you know my mother?'

'It is a long tale, are you sure you are ready to hear it?'

I scoff. 'How did you get in here?'

William's brows furrow. 'I travelled with aid of my patron.'

I raise an eyebrow. 'Patron?'

He hands me the soup and a spoon. Ladling up the soup, I raise the spoon to my lips and take a sip.

'A warlock makes a pact with an elemental being such as salamanders or sylphs and then are attributed special abilities. My own pact is with a salamander, and so I received protection against fire.'

My eyes narrow. 'Sure. Now how do you know my mother?'

'Patience is a virtue. Listen a little while. I know you are in a state of befuddlement, but I shall loosen the haze around your memories.' He takes the bowl from me and clicks his fingers. The contents in the bowl disappear as if the container had been cleansed with soap and water. 'You are not from this time. My own year of birth is 1701. I was born to a stablemaster and his wife in the court of the Grand High Wizard Fulke the Barbarous. Fulke was known for experiments on your people and many passed away.' William gulps. 'Fulke took a liking to a witch princess named Myrtle and showered her with lavish gifts.

They married and soon a babe was born in 1702, and the terrible nature of the wizard soon shone forth. Myrtle tried to escape, but she was young and her powers untrained. Fleeing with the aid of my father, the stablemaster, we journeyed for three years; your ma's nose often in an ancient tome. Eventually, she learnt one could travel through time. If she traded powers to another and built a garden like the one in the tome, Fulke would be betwixt time until she passed away.'

William caresses my face, and I shiver. 'Don't touch me.'

Pain pierces his eyes, but he removes the hand. 'Your ma took you to a different time, it seems.' He pulls a crumpled letter from his pocket. 'These are the instructions given to me. Your ma gave your hand in marriage to me when you were four and I was five. We were close as children, and I was to protect you from Fulke.' William smiles and puffs out his chest. 'Upon adulthood, I entered the sorcery guild funded by the pouch of silver your ma handed to me when you were six, before you both entered a swirling silver vortex as bells chimed.'

'This is ridiculous. You need to leave.'

The ground beneath us rumbles. The silver bell in the yard rings with ear-splitting intensity. *Crack.* The window splits and is pulled out by some horrific, unseen force, splintering the walls. The glass shatters and catches the late afternoon sunlight as it falls to the ground.

A tall, imposing figure in purple robes strides through the devastation. His blue eyes, similar to mine, flash with anger as he strokes his long, white beard. His long, white hair spirals over his shoulder tied in a long plait. His sharply pointed ears stand out.

William grabs my hand and pulls me in the opposite direction. We hurtle down the hallway as he tugs open the door and hurries outside. 'You now bear witness to the power of Fulke, your father.'

Boom. William throws himself to the ground, sheltering my body with his own. He rolls me out of the way, my breath trembling in my throat as my heart nearly pauses. Wood is flung around us as I glance towards the shack now torn asunder.

'Do you believe now?' William stands and draws me to my feet.

'Daughter, where is your mother?' Fulke yells, pointing a finger in my direction. 'You must all die for the crime of treason: stealing my precious tome.'

William's eyes lower and I follow the direction of his gaze; the tome.

'*Fatable fatalis,*' cries Fulke.

'Dive for your inheritance.' Willian leaps forward, blocking my path as a wave of fire shoots from the wizard's hand. I drop to a crouch. Running low, I dash forward, pick up the tome and make my way behind the man who just saved my life. He must be badly hurt. I stand up.

William's clothes are engulfed in flames, but he does not appear to burn as he cranes his head over his shoulder and smiles. 'You should flee. Page seventeen.' He reaches his hand into a pocket and tosses me a tiny silver bell.

'What about you?' My lower lip trembles.

'Flee.' William glows blue and turns back to his opponent. He clasps his hands together in a triangle. *'Electra holdaris.'*

Fulke is surrounded in blue light and lifted off the ground. He flails, like a fish out of water, the sky streaked with orange and pink as the sun drops below the horizon. 'When did you become powerful?'

My stomach churns as the impossibility of this scenario gathers my insides in a knot. I turn and bolt, tears streaming down my face as the grief of my mother's passing nearly swallows me whole, and the absurdity of this situation defies logic. I sprint down the hill to the beach and collapse to my knees on the sand. I open the book, thumbing the well-read pages, my body shaking until I reach page seventeen. Scanning the page, I read the instructions.

Spell for unlocking lost memories
One should not travel oft through time as children for you shall inherit an unsound mind, locking away your memories. One can regain their memories by ringing a silver bell,

knee deep in briny water, and casting to the
old ones these words ...

I step into the ocean, my breath catching as the cold flows through me. When I am knee high, I ring the bell before I speak. 'Clear my fog, old ones. I am forever grateful as you unlock my scattered memories.'

A rush of air passes through me. I close my eyes as pain gathers behind my pupils, and I let out a gasp. Pictures form in my mind. My heart thuds dully before it speeds up. Love and joy fill me along with memories of my mother teaching me to fly on a broom, and of her trying to cure my cold with some strange concoction.

When I felt blue she would summon fairies into the room to dance and make me laugh. Memories, of William and I playing and eating together, of me vowing I would marry William in that childish way all children play at, comes crashing in. Then my first memory of cruel words, raised voices and barely concealed threats in that hideous voice of my father, an ancient elf. His non-human heart barely held enough love for my human mother, leaving no love left for me. Shivering, I step out of the water and flick through the book, looking for anything that may help.

Portal Timeus

My eyes fly over the paper. Getting the gist, I turn and sprint up the hill to see Fulke striding towards me, dragging William behind him.

'Daughter.' His jaw clenches. 'Relinquish the artifact and you may yet live.' He gives me a cruel smile. 'Power has passed from mother to daughter. My wife is dead.'

I nod. 'Yes.'

He dumps William unceremoniously, before tossing his braid back over his shoulder. His eyes narrow and lock on mine. 'You shall make an excellent test subject.'

'Leave me alone.' I take a step back.

He clucks his tongue before he gives me a cold smile. 'Your flesh is my flesh. Part elf, part human. I will suck you dry of all your power.' He traces a circle in the air; it glows faintly before his starts mumbling.

'Mary,' William groans. 'Help.'

I sprint directly at Fulke and shove him aside as he tries to grab my clothes. Diving on to William, the tome and bell clutched in my hand. I ring it and recite the incantation. '*Portalis—*'

'A date,' William mutters.

'*Portalis nineteen fifty-seven timeus.*' I ring the bell.

'No,' roars Fulke as William and I are engulfed in a silvery vortex. Bells chime around us.

We land with an 'oof' on that familiar sandy beach. I loose a shuddering breath as I realise we are in the same place.

'Same place, different time.' William groans as he sits up. 'Time travel is complicated. One travels to a set date and hour in the location they currently occupy. From there you can travel across the Earth in that time and encounter the events occurring.'

'Are we safe?'

William shakes his head. 'Nay. Fulke will stalk us until that tome is in his keeping. You are a bonus.'

'How can we stop him?'

'Train and read the tome until you become familiar with its knowledge. Grow a garden like your mother's then he can no longer follow and you will be safe and happy.' William stands and pulls me up, before releasing my hand. 'You will be safe for a while and I yearn for my home.'

'Are you leaving me?'

William smiles. 'This is not my time. My clothes and manner betrays my ancient ways.'

I swallow the sob that threatens to spill out of me. 'Would you leave your time if I gave you a reason to?'

A flush spreads across his cheeks. 'Fulke knows my magical signature. He will chase me and leave you alone.'

I close the gap between us and press a kiss to his cheek. As I draw away, he places a hand on the spot. 'Do you mean to travel with and be my bride?'

I smile. 'If you wouldn't mind.'

'You do not yet know the wonders of the old world before humankind wiped most of them from the Earth.

You shall smile when you first see a dragon or unicorn.' My eyes widen as William takes my hand and incites the spell. '*Portalis seventeen thirty-one timeus.*'

As I ring the bell, a vortex appears in front of us. *Crack.* I glance over my shoulder, my father steps out of a shimmering rip in time.

'He travels freely without magical tools.' William grabs my hand and sprints towards the portal. 'My parents will love you.'

'I will follow you until the end of time.' Fulke rushes after us as we step into the portal.

I turn and glare at my father as our bodies begin to shimmer. 'I will find a way to stop you.'

His malicious laughter erupts behind us as we disappear.

The End.

Also by Ima Ghoul

Zombies & Papercuts

Would you believe it I am Would you believe it I am thirty-three and have never been pashed? Let me introduce myself, my name is Alara and I am a librarian in a small country town in South Australia and a local nobody. As my luck would have it, doom coincides with my birthday and the party guests happen to be zombies.

But I am an eternal optimist. Will today be the day I finally share my first kiss? Armed only with my wit and books let's hope I don't get a papercut. They hurt more than a zombie bite.

Weird & Wacky Anthology: Volume One

Delve into the the wacky, the witty and mildly creepy, from tales of magic, aliens and ghouls to sweet romances.

Ima Ghoul, author of Zombies and Papercuts, brings the adventurous reader an anthology of short stories that won't fail to tantalise and amuse.

Will you cross the threshold?

Turn the page ... I dare you!

Zombies & Cricket

The night fills with the familiar chirp of crickets and the irritating hum of mozzies. I swat at one. My chest tightens as I lick my lips, trying to will away the intrusive thought, and now guilty pleasure, of wondering if mozzies have edible brains. So, it is happening, and relatively fast.

After the zombie apocalypse, the government found a temporary solution and encouraged us to continue living our lives. Let me introduce myself. My name is Gavin, a 43-year-old cattle farmer from South Australia, with a love of cricket. As the one—year anniversary—now aptly named Use Your Noggin Day—and my gal's birthday, approaches, there has been an increase in zombie attacks.

Will I be able to protect Alara, keep my humanity and still play the match next weekend?